THE
PAINTED
CHEST

To my mum and dad for their abiding love and encouragement.

"Beware the barrenness of a busy life."
Socrates

Library and Archives Canada Cataloguing in Publication

Mills, Judith
    The painted chest / Judith Christine Mills.

ISBN-13: 978-1-55263-015-0 , ISBN-10: 1-55263-015-3 (bound)
ISBN-13: 978-1-55263-809-5 , ISBN-10: 1-55263-809-X (pbk.)

    I. Title.

PS8576.I571P34 1999   jC813'.54   C98-932740-X

The publisher gratefully acknowledges the support of the Canada Council for the Arts and the Ontario Arts Council for its publishing program. We acknowledge the support of the Government of Ontario through the Ontario Media Development Corporation's Ontario Book Initiative.

We acknowledge the financial support of the Government of Canada through the Book Publishing Industry Development Program (BPIDP) for our publishing activities.

Key Porter kids is an imprint of
Key Porter Books Limited
Six Adelaide Street East, Tenth Floor
Toronto, Ontario
Canada M5C 1H6
www.keyporter.com

Design and electronic formatting: Kathryn Moore

Printed and bound in China

07 08 09 10 11 6 5 4 3 2 1

In the chill of early dawn, the villagers rose from their beds to begin another long day.

They did not notice the clusters of wildflowers that struggled to face the sun.

They did not hear the sweet morning songs of the birds.

Exchanging solemn nods and few words, they made their way down the tracks to plots of corn and barley, cabbages and potatoes. They traveled quickly, their wooden carts creaking and rattling along the uneven ground.

Maddie followed her father's cart, her younger brother, Luke, by her side. A bright white pebble glistened in the sun. Maddie stooped to touch it. But quickly, for the push of the crowd behind them soon sent her scurrying to catch up.

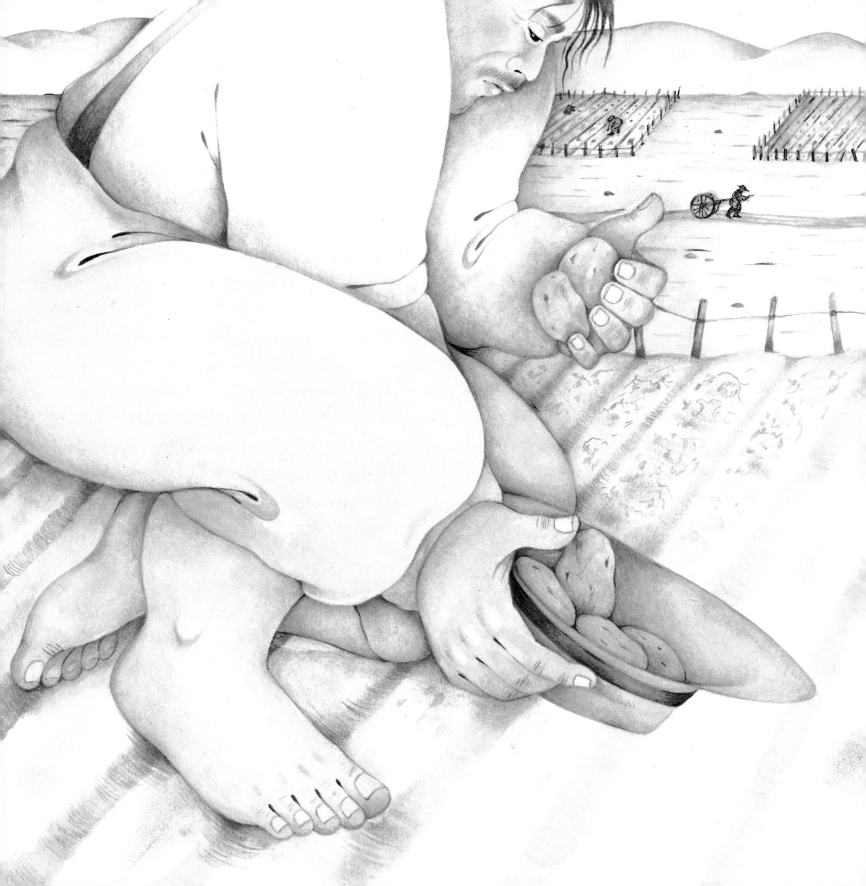

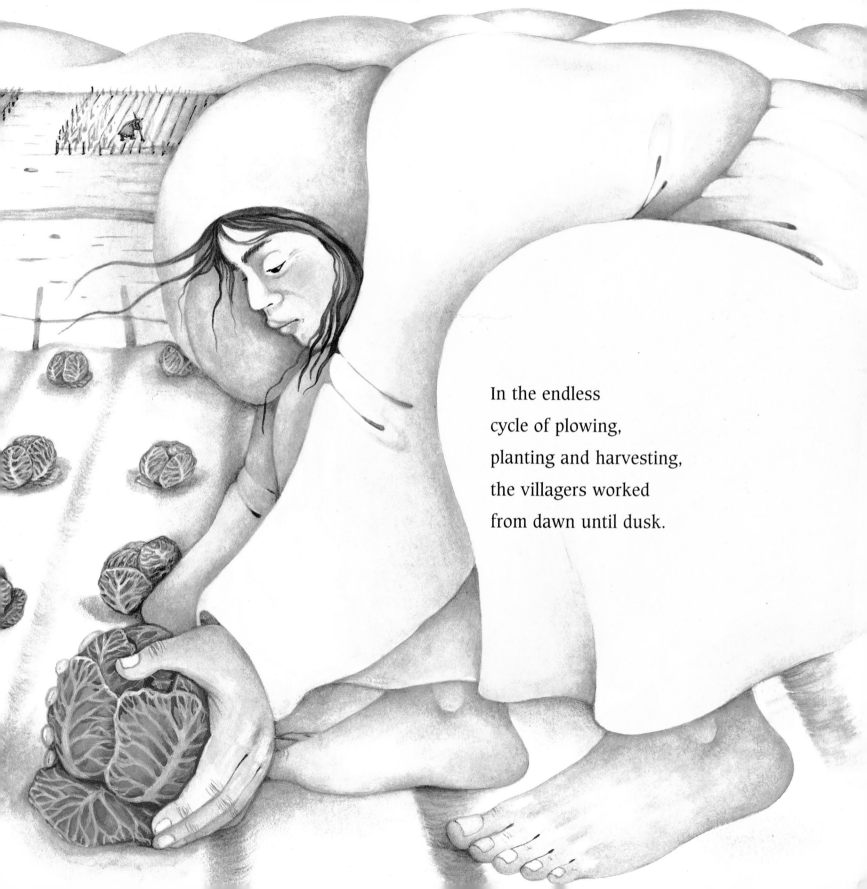

In the endless
cycle of plowing,
planting and harvesting,
the villagers worked
from dawn until dusk.

Tired and weary at the close of each day, the villagers returned home. And as the moon rose in the evening and a million stars danced and twinkled above, they did not look skyward to ponder or imagine, but fell exhausted into their beds. Though their larders were full, their nights were empty of dreams.

Maddie had lived in the village for as long as she could remember. It was the only world she'd ever known. But for all its abundance of sun, rain, soil and crops, Maddie could not keep from longing for more.

On the days when old Geordie, the oldest inhabitant of the village, was too frail to tend his crops, Maddie would take him cabbages, corn, and a few potatoes. In return, he would tell her of the great famine that had struck the village many years before. Then, the daily struggle to survive had overshadowed all else.

Sometimes Maddie would tell Luke the stories she'd heard from old Geordie. Others had long since dismissed him, but Maddie found his words fascinating.

Sometimes Maddie would awaken at night and gaze out the window to where the fields lay bathed in moonlight. She wondered about the people who had lived before the famine, and the kind of world that they had lived in.

One day, while clearing rocks from the fields, the villagers unearthed a large object caked in mud.

It was an old wooden chest with big brass handles and a rounded lid secured with a rusty lock.

Layers of dirt were swirled from the chest with a wet rag to reveal strange designs and an inscription. Old Geordie hesitated until Maddie gave him a gentle shove. She knew that only he might know what the chest was trying to tell them.

"A precious treasure lies within,
Rich beyond imagining.
For those who seek a better day,
The pure of heart must lead the way.
The days will all be long and cold,
If you nourish body but not soul.
There's more to life than flesh and bone,
We cannot live by bread alone."

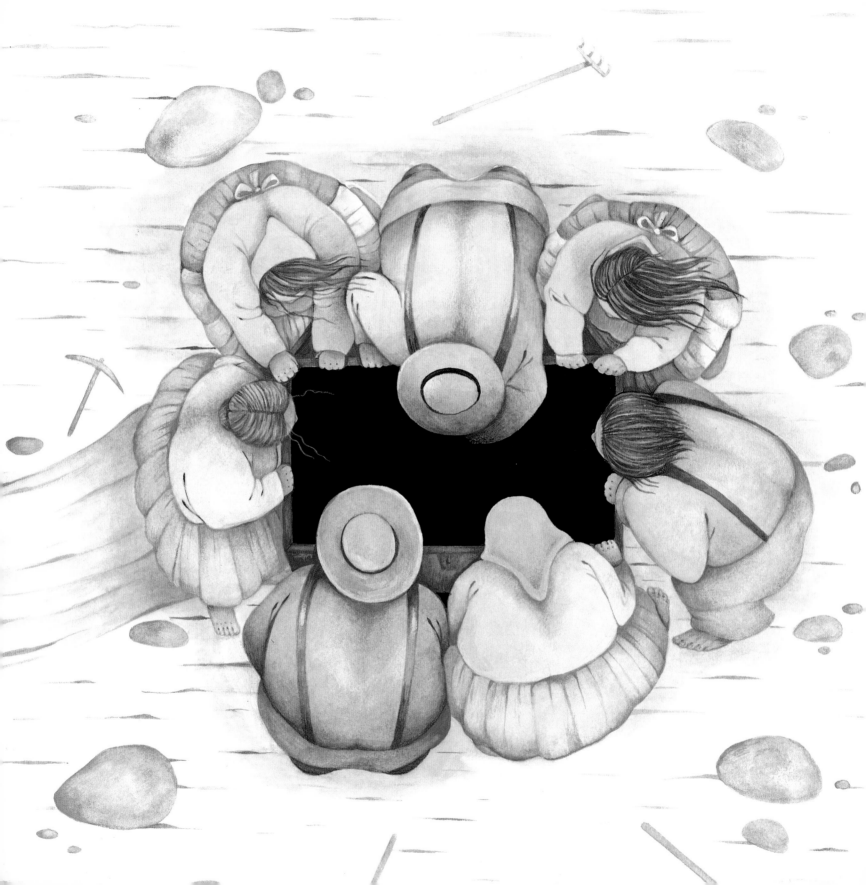

With the promise of treasure before them, the villagers quickly broke the chest's lock and flung the lid wide open.

Inside were long silver-colored pipes, oddly shaped objects of metal, wood and string and many pairs of strange, flimsy shoes. The villagers rummaged hopefully for a while, but soon closed the lid and threw the chest onto a pile of rocks.

Disappointed, they picked up their tools and returned to work.

Old Geordie had not moved an inch or spoken a word since
the chest was first opened. Maddie was sure she could see tears in
his eyes when she took his arm and led him home.

When Maddie fell asleep that night, the painted chest and the strange things within it filled her dreams.

Before the village awoke, she slipped from her bed and returned to the fields. She might never have found her way in that time of dark shapes and shadows, but the chest cast a soft glow in the half-light, and she climbed the rocks towards it. Over and over, Maddie tried to pull the chest free, but she could not do it alone.

Later in the day, while the villagers worked the lower fields, Maddie gathered as many of the other children as she could. With Luke scrambling close behind, she quietly led them to the abandoned chest.

Pulling together now, they moved the chest up the slope to the hills and far from view.

Maddie opened the lid and gently lifted the objects out, laying them on the grass before her. She studied the figures upon the chest very carefully, then handed an object to each of the children. After handing out the strange shoes, too, Maddie placed a pair upon her own feet and lifted one of the wooden pipes to her lips.

Moments before, the only noise had been the rustle of the wind. Now there was another sound, faint at first but growing louder. Workers paused in their fields, dropping their tools to the ground. They stood motionless, hypnotized by the sweet, lilting sound that drifted across them like a soft, warm blanket.

Flocks of birds gathered and began to answer the music from the hills.
And for the first time in a very long time, the villagers gazed
skyward and heard their song, too.

In the days that followed, a different world began to unfold. Joy
spread throughout the valley and everything the villagers looked
upon was transformed. The fields, no longer pale and muted,
shimmered gold, orange and crimson. Wildflowers that once lay
unnoticed began to flourish and a beautiful fragrance filled the air.

Once the villagers began to nurture their gardens with more than sun, water and soil, they found they did not have to spend each moment toiling. Strangely, there was time now to stop and smile, to talk with each other and to watch the children play.

Music and dancing, laughter and color became such a great part of the villagers' lives they could not begin to imagine how they had ever lived without it.